Hi, I'm Tom

And your name is ... -------------------

12

Winning Isn't Everything!

Jennifer Moore-Mallinos
Illustrations: Marta Fàbrega

SENTENCES I OFTEN HEAR

Mom and Dad are always talking to me about being a good sport, about knowing how to win and how to lose. Sentences about good sportsmanship are always floating around, regardless of the game I play. Be it a board game, card game, video game or even a sport like hockey, as long as I show good sportsmanship in any of them, Mom and Dad are happy.

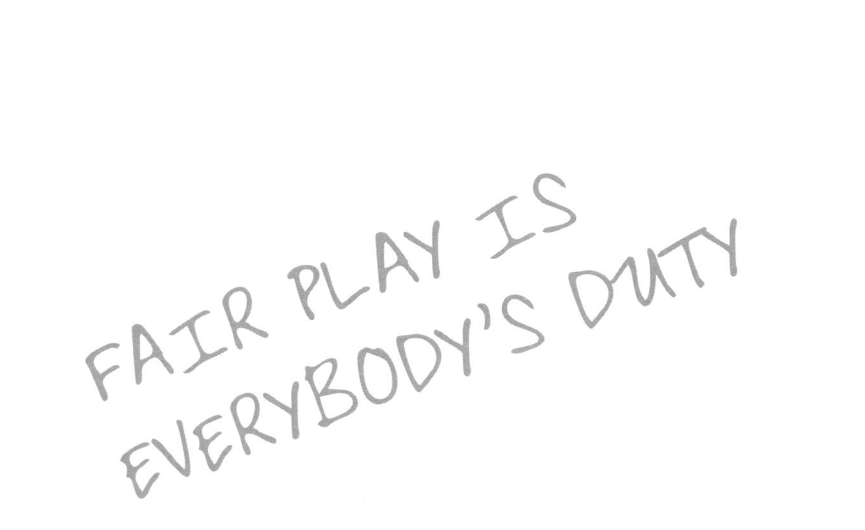

Although I hear it all the time, I never really thought about what it means to be a good sport until the last hockey game of the season. That's when I learned that being a good sport not only included the players but everyone else, too!

THE MOMENT HAD ARRIVED!

This wasn't just any game…it was for the championship! It was almost game time, and everyone was so excited! Of course, we all wanted to win, including me!

BEFORE THE GAME

A SPEECH IN THE LOCKER ROOM

While our families and friends were busy finding seats, the team was getting ready in the locker room and talking about winning. Coach stood up, cleared his throat, and waited for everyone to stop talking. As usual, Coach reminded us about playing by the rules and playing fair.

2 WINNING ISN'T EVERYTHING

Coach said that it was natural for us to want to win the championship for our school, but he reminded us that it wasn't about winning or losing but how we played the game. Trying our best and having fun and doing it honestly was what really counted. We all agreed.

TO THE RINK!

It was finally game time! We gathered in a circle in the middle of the locker room and shouted our team cheer, then grabbed our sticks and headed for the rink. I was the last player in line, and I couldn't wait to get out there. Just as I was about to step onto the ice, I felt a tap on my shoulder. I turned around and saw one of the parents from the other team facing me. He looked angry and was wagging his finger in my face.

10

The parent told me that our team better watch out because no matter what it took, his son's team was going to win the championship. Luckily, just then, Coach showed up beside me. He told me to get onto the ice and then turned to the parent whose finger was still wagging in the air and asked him to go find a seat.

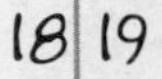

...AND VERY BAD MANNERS

But before the parent left, Coach warned him that just like the players, all spectators were expected to be good sports. Coach told him that if he continued to make threats and behave in such an ugly way, he would be asked to leave the arena. The parent laughed and then disappeared into the stands.

AN ANGRY AND AGGRESSIVE ATTITUDE

The game was tied at two-to-two! There were five minutes left in the game! The crowd was out of their seats, clapping and cheering. I looked up into the crowd, and spotted that same angry parent coming down the stairs. He went straight over to the rink. He looked really mad, and he started yelling, “Take them down! Go and get ’em!”

EVERYBODY GOT UPSET

Until now, both teams were playing fairly, and everyone seemed to be having a good time. Then everything changed. First, the pushing started and next the shoving. Some of the players started jabbing one another with their sticks. The louder that parent yelled, the rougher the fighting became. All the fun was gone.

With seconds left in the game, the referee blew his whistle. At first the crowd booed, but then the arena filled with silence. At the far end of the rink, a player was lying face down on the ice. He wasn't moving! With all the confusion, nobody, including the angry parent noticed that it was his son who was hurt.

A TERRIBLE OUTCOME!
AND THE GAME WAS STOPPED

AM 12

AT THE END, WE ALL AGREED

The parent sat on the ice clinging to his son. We all gathered around, anxiously waiting for the ambulance to arrive. At that moment, we all agreed that it was okay to want to win, but it wasn't okay to try to win by playing rough, cheating, or showing poor sportsmanship. With tears in his eyes, the father apologized for his behavior. He acknowledged that perhaps winning wasn't so necessary after all, that trying to do one's best and having fun was what's truly important.

WINNING ISN'T EVERYTHING

The ambulance arrived and the player was taken to the hospital. The referee blew his whistle to let us know that there were still a few seconds left in the game, but nobody moved. Winning the championship just wasn't important anymore.

15

PLAYING FAIR ISN'T ALWAYS EASY

The game stayed tied at two-to-two, so nobody won the championship. It didn't matter. What mattered most was that a player broke his arm because we forgot how to play fair. We wanted to win so badly that being a good sport wasn't important anymore. Being sportsmanlike is not always easy, even for adults, but as long as we have someone like Coach and our parents to remind us, then all we need to do is to play fair and have a good time.

Activities

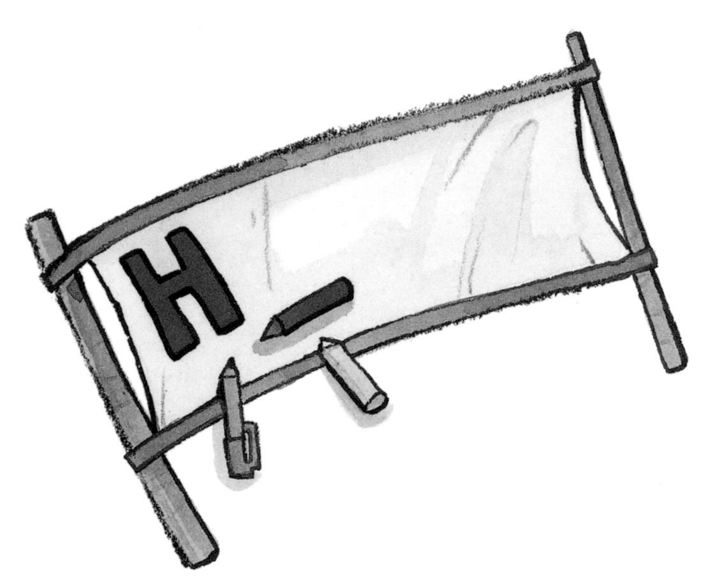

TEAM BANNER OR SIGN

For a banner, cut paper, poster board, cardboard, or fabric to desired length. Using large letters, perhaps bubble-shaped so that your message can be seen from afar, print your team name or write encouraging words on the banner. For example; "Go team, Go!" or "Hooray, Tigers!" Fill in the words with colored markers and use glitter to make it more visible.

If you want to make a sign, attach your banner to one or two pieces of wood so you can hold it up. Your message should show your good sportsmanship. Have fun!

TROPHIES AND MEDALS

When a person or a team is given a trophy or a medal it means that they have done a great job. Parents, grandparents, teachers, and coaches all love to be reminded that they have done a good thing and that they are appreciated. What better way to show those special people your appreciation than by giving them their very own personalized trophy or medal!

To make a medal, look for a piece of cardboard and, with an adult to help you, cut a circle. Look for a piece of aluminum foil and cut it into tiny pieces. Glue the pieces to the cardboard until it is shiny all over. Next, with a marker, write something special on your medal. It can be as simple as "#1." Poke a small hole in the top of your medal. Cut yarn or string to desired length. Put the yarn or string through the hole of the medal and tie a knot. You may want to decorate your medal with glitter or sparkles. And for extra fun, you might want to make a trophy or medal for yourself, too!

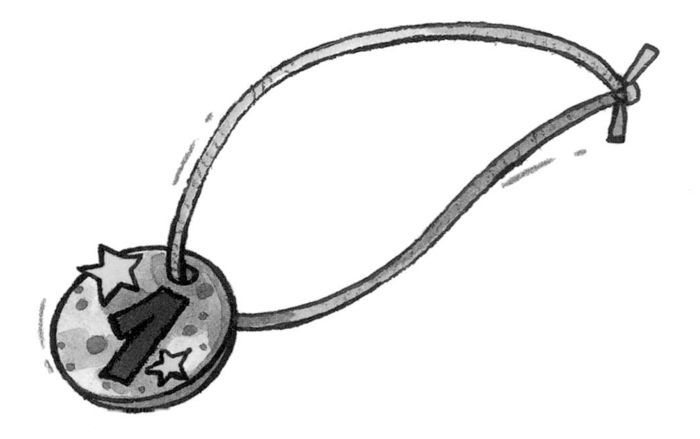

YOURSELF, LIFE-SIZE

Being part of a team means spending a lot of time practicing and playing games. How about decorating the locker room with life-size posters of each member of your team! Or you could make a poster of yourself and hang it in your bedroom!

To make the poster you will need a roll of paper, about 3 feet wide and 5 feet long, which you can buy at an arts and crafts store. Roll out the paper onto the floor and lie down on it. Ask a friend to trace around your entire body, and cut out the figure along the traced line. Complete the poster by drawing your hair, eyes, and so on. Dress the figure by drawing on your team uniform. Color the figure with markers, crayons or colored pencils.

When you have completed coloring, use a marker to write words or phrases that describe you as a player or teammate. For example, if your poster is of you in a hockey uniform, you may describe yourself as fast, tireless, and a good shooter.

DESIGN YOUR OWN GAME

Do you have a good idea for a game? It could be a board game, a card game, or even a different way to play a game or sports activity that already exists. All you need is your imagination and creativity! Once you have an idea for a new game, you are ready to get started.

Write down the objective of the game and a set of rules or instructions of how the game is played.

If you are designing a new board game, make a list of all the materials (player pieces, dice, and so on) that you will need to make a good game.

First, make a board game out of cardboard. Starting from beginning to end, draw each space onto your board. It's always fun to add directions for some of the spaces. For example, if you land on the third space you may ask the player to move ahead two spaces.

Designing a new card game or sports activity can also be fun. Remember to play fair when you play your game!

Note to parents

We all have a desire to win. Winning feels good! There is a sense of accomplishment when we win, and when our children win we feel more accomplished as parents. Perhaps this is why many of us are sometimes overly enthusiastic when it comes to "supporting" our child's participation in a game, especially when the team is winning.

No matter what kind of game we play, whether it's a card game, a soccer match, a hockey game or even participating in a raffle, we all want to win. For many of us, our initial intention of playing any game is solely for enjoyment. However, our competitiveness can sometimes take over in a negative way. For both players and spectators, the consequence of behavior that lacks sportsmanship takes the enjoyment out of the game. It only takes one poor sport to ruin the game!

Most of us have experienced, at some time of our lives, the feeling associated with losing. We would probably all agree that losing never feels good; it's unpleasant, disappointing and often disheartening. Knowing that we tried our hardest to win does not always make us feel better, and that is why it is so hard to convince our children that competing with honesty is more important than winning. It may be hard, but it is necessary.

If the desire to win becomes overwhelming and affects our sportsmanlike behavior, it's time for some self-examination! After all, our children model our actions even more than our words! We are not only teaching them the rules of the game, but also the rules for living.

The purpose of this book is not only to remind parents about the importance of good sportsmanship, but to teach children that good sportsmanlike behavior includes everyone… players, coaches, and spectators alike.

We know that we can't win all the time, but it's certainly fun trying. As long as everybody is having fun and playing fairly and safe, nobody loses!

WINNING ISN'T EVERYTHING!

First edition for the United States and Canada published in 2007 by Barron's Educational Series, Inc.

Title of the original in Spanish: *¡Ganar no es todo!*

Text: Jennifer Moore-Mallinos
Illustrations: Marta Fàbrega

All inquiries should be addressed to:
Barron's Educational Series, Inc.
250 Wireless Boulevard
Hauppauge, New York 11788
http://www.barronseduc.com

ISBN-13: 978-0-7641-3791-4
ISBN-10: 0-7641-3791-3

Library of Congress Control Number: 2007922275

Printed in China
9 8 7 6 5 4 3 2 1